FRIENDS
OF ACPL

S0-CID-636

SARAH WINNEMUCCA

By Doris Kloss

DILLON PRESS, INC.
MINNEAPOLIS, MINNESOTA

© 1981 by Dillon Press, Inc. All rights reserved

Dillon Press, Inc., 500 South Third Street
Minneapolis, Minnesota 55415

Printed in the United States of America

Library of Congress Cataloging in Publication Data

Kloss, Doris.
  Sarah Winnemucca.

  (The story of an American Indian)
  SUMMARY: Recounts the life of the influential Paiute woman who
rescued several hundred of her people held captive during the Bannock
War.
  1. Hopkins, Sarah Winnemucca, 1844?-1891—Juvenile literature. 2.
Paiute, Indians—Biography—Juvenile literature. [1. Hopkins, Sarah
Winnemucca, 1844?-1891. 2. Paiute Indians—Biography. 3. Indians of
North America—Biography] I. Title.
E99.P2K56   970.004'97 [B] [92]   81-390
ISBN 0-87518-178-3   AACR1

SARAH WINNEMUCCA

Sarah Winnemucca (1844?-1891) was the child and grandchild of chiefs, and she was also made a chief of the Northern Paiutes. This honor was given to her in recognition of the fact that she rescued several hundred of her people held captive during the Bannock War.

Her life spanned the time in which white settlers took over the Northern Paiute homeland in western Nevada. No longer able to follow their old way of life, the Paiutes suffered much hardship on the reservations where they were forced to stay. A brilliant speaker and fearless writer, Sarah Winnemucca brought their suffering to the attention of the American people.

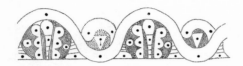

Contents

I STRANGERS COME
   TO THE BIG MEADOW   page 5

II OVER THE MOUNTAINS   page 17

III A WISE MAN DIES   page 27

IV HELP FROM THE ARMY   page 36

V A NEW WAY OF LIFE   page 43

VI ARMY SCOUT   page 51

VII BROKEN PROMISES   page 62

VIII THE STORY IS TOLD   page 69

CHAPTER I

Strangers Come to the Big Meadow

The Great Basin was a bleak and barren place. It was almost entirely encircled by mountains. Narrow, jagged mountains rising almost a mile above the basin floor cut it up into many small valleys. Plants and animals were few. Desert-loving plants like sagebrush, greasewood, and creosote covered the dry earth. Porcupine and rye grasses grew on mountain slopes, and above them juniper and willow trees stretched their branches skyward. High above on the upper slopes stood forests of piñon trees.

When Sarah Winnemucca was born in 1844, her people, the Northern Paiutes, were living as they had since they first came to their homeland long, long ago. No one knows for sure when they first came to the Great Basin. Scientists believe that their ancestors were among the last groups of people to cross the land bridge that connected North America with Asia at the end of the Ice Age, ten thousand years ago. They tried to stay near what water there was in their desert home, and that is how they got their name. Paiute comes from two words: *pah,* which means "water," and *ute,* a word for "this way." In the Great Basin, they kept to the land around the Humboldt, Carson, and Walker river sinks, where the rivers seemed to disappear into the earth.

The homeland of the Northern Paiutes.

Life was hard for the Northern Paiutes. Their land in western Nevada was locked in by the snow-capped Sierra Nevada mountain range on the west and the waterless desert on the east. They could not farm because the summers were so hot and dry, and there was almost no rainfall except in the mountains. Biting frosts came early in the fall and late in the spring, and the winters were bitterly cold.

For three seasons of the year the Northern Paiutes spent their days roaming the Great Basin in search of food. They traveled from valley to lake, to mountain slopes, and along rivers and streams.

Everyone in the family worked. Children and old people

gathered seeds, nuts, and firewood. The women harvested plant foods and made baskets and clothing. Men and boys hunted rabbits and squirrels and fished and netted ducks.

As soon as the first green leaves began to appear on the plants in the marshes, families left their winter lodges to begin their search for food. Since there was not enough food and water for many people in one place, they traveled in bands of a few families.

The lush meadow at Humboldt Sink—a low, marshy area on the Humboldt River—was a favorite place. When they camped at the Big Meadow in the early spring, they gathered the tender shoots of cattail and squaw cabbage.

Mothers would wade into the marsh and pull the fresh cattails from the mud. Peeling the brown soggy leaves off, they fed the white spears to their hungry children huddled on the bank. The fresh green food was a real treat after eating only dried berries, seeds, roots, and dried fish and meat all winter.

Men collected bird eggs tucked among the tall reeds in the marshes. Pushing small rafts with poles, they weaved in and out among the tall grass to find the eggs, putting them in small baskets. Their rafts, like their baskets, were made from rushes that grew in the marshes. These were the only boats they had, for there was no wood of the kind that could be used to make canoes.

In May, when the fish began to spawn in the Truckee and Walker rivers, families gathered from miles away for a fishing festival. Some years fish were so plentiful that the young boys could scoop them up in their arms. Sometimes they stayed at fishing camps for weeks, feasting, having prayer dances, and playing games. They dried strips of fish on racks for the winter.

There was no let-up in their search for food. During the spring and summer, women and children picked berries, seeds, and dug roots while the men hunted for the small animals that lived there. If word came that the berry of the desert thorn was ripe and plentiful in a valley fifty miles away, off they went to pick the berries before the birds and ground squirrels ate them up.

As they roamed the great desert, they built shelters as they needed them. At nightfall they laid brushes across two bushes to make a shelter large enough for one person to crawl under. If the family expected to stay in a place for

Pine nuts, shown here in a Paiute winnowing tray, were an important food.

several weeks, the women piled sagebrush in a circle shoulder-high. These shelters broke the wind and were quite warm.

The Paiutes were always careful to leave some green plants and seeds for the following season. They believed that when they took something from the earth, they should leave something in return. If they had nothing to give, they left a rock or stone. No one picked up these offerings, for that would have been stealing.

In the fall they climbed the mountain slopes to gather pine nuts from the piñon, or pine nut, trees. The pine nut was the main food in their diet, and it was very important for them to gather as many as they could to store for the winter. Before going to the mountains, they gathered together to hold a prayer dance. All night long they danced shoulder to shoulder in a large circle around a small pine nut tree and sang songs about the wind, clouds, and animals.

As they climbed toward the stands of pine nut trees, they filled their water jugs from the mountain springs. These small jugs were tightly woven baskets covered with pitch to make them watertight. The men beat the pine nuts off the trees with poles while the women and children gathered them in large baskets. The pine nuts were roasted and ground into flour, which was mixed with water to make a hearty gruel, or mush.

Rabbits provided much of the Paiutes' clothing and what little meat they had as well. The hides of deer and antelope were hard to come by, but rabbits were plentiful in the Great Basin. It took many strips of the little skins to make a blanket. During the day the people wore the blankets as capes and curled up in them at night.

As winter approached, several bands gathered for a rabbit drive. Long nets were stretched across desert bushes in a semicircle to hem in the rabbits so that they could be killed quickly.

Everyone looked forward to the rabbit drives because it was one of the few times of the year when people from different bands could get together. Young people courted, and one and all sang and played games. The rabbit drives, fishing festivals, and the pine nut festival were the only ceremonies the Paiutes held. Food was too scarce in the Great Basin for the large gatherings that other Indian people enjoyed.

When the first snow fell, each family returned to their own winter camp near the marshes. The sites for these camps were carefully chosen near a spring that would not freeze over and where there was plenty of firewood.

If the supply of wood ran out, the family left the shelter

and built a new one. It was easier than going great distances to gather firewood, for they had no tools for cutting down trees or sawing wood.

One of the first chores a child was given was gathering firewood. Having enough fuel for winter was so important that it was part of a young girl's ceremony when she became a woman. Each day the girl gathered and stacked five piles of wood. Five was a sacred number among the Paiutes. A girl who gathered large piles of wood would make a good wife, and her family would stay warm.

To withstand the winter's cold, the Paiutes built snug shelters called wickiups that looked something like big overturned baskets. They were made of cattail mats laced to a framework of juniper and willow poles. Reeds, grasses, and brush covered the roof because the Paiutes had few large animal skins. Inside, mats of woven rushes covered the earth floor, and around the walls were piles of soft grass for sitting and sleeping on.

The women repaired the old wickiups or built new ones while the men collected the food they had stored in pits during the year. During the winter that followed, the family huddled around the fire. Men made nets and tools, and the women wove baskets and made clothing. Old people snoozed in their rabbit skin blankets by the fire and told their grandchildren stories about the wind and animals.

The Northern Paiutes were hard working and peace loving. They shared the places where they gathered food and hunted with other Indian people in the Great Basin. They had no war chiefs or warriors, for their endless search for food kept them too busy to fight among themselves or with their neighbors.

A wickiup, the winter home of a Paiute family.

Their tribal leader was chosen not only for leadership ability but also because of knowledge of where the best sources of food could be found. At the time of Sarah's birth, the leader of the Northern Paiutes was Chief Winnemucca, Sarah's grandfather.

Chief Winnemucca was a wise and kind leader. He was an excellent hunter and knew where to find the best game, when the mudhens and ducks returned to the marshes, and the best places to gather growing plants. He was concerned about the welfare of his people. He wanted them to live happily and peacefully with their white brothers who were just now coming across their desert lands.

That the few white trappers he had seen were long-lost brothers of his people, he did not doubt. According to an old, old story, which Chief Winnemucca firmly believed, the world was started by a couple and their four children living in a beautiful forest. One day the children quarreled bitterly, and their father ordered them to separate and go across the ocean. The dark couple strode off in one direction and the white pair in the other. The white boy and girl were never heard from again, but the myth promised that one day they would return.

Nevertheless, Chief Winnemucca was worried when the Murphy-Stevens-Townsend wagon train camped in the Big Meadow above Humboldt Sink in October 1844. The meadow was a well-loved camping place of the Paiutes. It was the one place in the huge desert where there was always some water. Chief Winnemucca watched anxiously as the white people's oxen, horses, and cattle drank that year's water supply. He was puzzled over why the men had come with their families.

Chief Winnemucca greeted the travelers, and with signs and drawings on the ground he learned that they were going to California. Since snow would soon begin falling, he offered to guide them across the Sierra Nevadas. The oxen pulled the wagons over the summit with chains. Only five of the eleven wagons made it to the other side, but it was an important event in history. These were the first wagons to cross the steep mountains, and soon many more would be following the trail over which Chief Winnemucca led the white people.

While he was guiding the wagon train, his daughter, Tuboitonie, gave birth to a little girl. It was during the pine nut season, and the child was born in a bark and rush wickiup where the family had their winter camp. She was named Somit-tone, or "Shellflower," for the pink-hued desert flower that blossomed in the spring. When she was twelve years old, she took the name of Sarah, the name we know her by today.

Sarah's father, Poito, was in charge of the Northern Paiutes while Chief Winnemucca was away, and the old chief returned only to leave soon again. This time he would go all the way to California.

The famous explorer, John Charles Frémont, was crossing Paiute lands. He was exploring the unknown West for the United States government. Chief Winnemucca met Frémont at Pyramid Lake. Eager to make his new friends feel welcome, he answered "Truckee, truckee," which means "all right," to everything they said. Frémont's party thought he was telling them his name. From then on, Chief Winnemucca was known among the whites as "Captain Truckee."

Led by Chief Winnemucca, Frémont and his men cross the mountains into the Sacramento Valley of California.

The Paiute chief and nine of his men guided the Frémont party over the same trail he had led the wagon train. Frémont and his men became so fond of their guide that they named a mountain stream and a lake "Truckee" in his honor. At Sutter's Fort in California, they learned about the war with Mexico. At the time California was a Mexican province and, unknown to the Paiutes, Mexico also claimed the Paiute homeland as its own. Chief Winnemucca served as an army scout for Frémont during the war and was a member of General Frémont's famous California Battalion.

Before he left, Chief Winnemucca had told Poito to try to keep peace with the white people crossing their lands. For a while this was not difficult. But, as word came that the Americans were winning the war against Mexico, the numbers of wagon trains headed for California increased. Soon, the would-be settlers hoped, California would become part of the United States. The strangers camped in the Big Meadow and let their horses and cattle graze, leaving no plants for the earth.

The travelers were tired from their long journey by the time they reached the Big Meadow. Fearful and distrustful, they fired at any Indians they happened to see. The Paiutes soon came to fear the blue-eyed, full-bearded strangers and their guns and rifles. Even a cloud of dust in the distance would cause mothers to hide their children until they were certain no wagon trains were coming.

As the meetings between whites and Indians grew more dangerous, Poito led the Northern Paiutes to the mountains for safety. They dug roots, picked berries, and hunted and fished while in the mountains. But, instead of storing their food in the usual pits, they piled it in large mounds and covered it with grass and rocks. A group of white people passing by set fire to the mounds of stored food. The Paiutes watched in horror as their entire winter supply of food went up in smoke.

CHAPTER II

Over the Mountains

When Chief Winnemucca returned from California at the end of the Mexican War, he was brimming over with tales of what he had seen. Sarah was only a toddler, but she was one of her grandfather's most eager listeners.

The old man said that the white people who lived on the other side of the mountains had big stone houses, large farms, and many tools. Their great ships sailed the ocean. The ships' bells and whistles made the most beautiful sounds he had ever heard. It was almost more than his wide-eyed audience could imagine.

Sometimes Chief Winnemucca dressed up in his army uniform with shiny brass buttons on the sleeves. In his soldier's clothes he would sing army songs and the "Star-Spangled Banner." The Paiutes loved to sing, and before long they were joining in. Among his most treasured belongings was a Bible in which General Frémont had written his name and a slip of paper which was actually a letter of recommendation from the general. It said, "Truckee is a trustworthy friend of the white people. I urge you to treat him as such."

Everyone was amazed that their chief's friends could talk to one another on paper. The Paiutes had no written

General John Charles Frémont.

language and their stories, history, and legends were passed on by word of mouth.

Chief Winnemucca continued to talk about his white friends. Finally, he told the tribe that he wanted them to go with him to California and see for themselves all the many wonderful things. This created a great deal of excitement in the camp. Every fall they gathered pine nuts on the slopes of the Sierra Nevadas but only a few of the strongest hunters had ever gone to the top of the mountains. Never to the other side.

They discussed the trip in council meetings and among themselves. Some thought that it would be good to see what it was like on the other side of the steep mountains. Others would have no part of it. They were content where they were, preferring their own way of life to that of the whites.

Sarah listened closely to the arguments. Her grandfather promised that they would be friends with the white people. Life would be much easier in California. They could farm and raise their own food. No longer would they have to be constantly on the move, combing the Great Basin for food. In California there was plenty of game and streams filled with fish, and they would not be disturbed.

This was a convincing reason for some. In years when there was little rainfall in the basin, there were few berries, roots, and seeds for the cold winter months. Sometimes the pine nut crop was not plentiful. Large animals had always been scarce.

Poito and many of the group weren't at all sure that they wanted to live near white people. They admired their wagons but were afraid of their guns. Even more frightening were the rumors that a party of white people trapped in the first snows in the Sierra Nevadas had eaten one another after their food ran out. Paiute mothers sometimes threatened to feed a child who misbehaved to the whites.

Sarah was relieved to hear her grandfather say this wasn't true. The group known as the Donner Party had stalled in the first heavy snowfall in 1846, but they died of starvation. They did not turn to cannibalism.

Eventually, Chief Winnemucca persuaded thirty families to go with him to California. He promised that he would bring them back home again if they were unhappy in the

new land. He insisted that Tuboitonie and her children—
Tom, Natchez, Mary, Sarah, and Elma—go with him. He
appointed Poito to take charge of those remaining in
Nevada. As before, he asked Poito to take care of his people
and to try to keep peace with the whites.

They held a feast the night before the families left for
California. They sang, danced, and played games. Prayers
were offered to the Spirit Father for a safe journey. There
was lots of weeping and hugging among families and
friends. In the book she later wrote, *Life Among the
Paiutes,* Sarah said that her feelings about going to
California were mixed. She wanted to live with her
grandfather's friends, and yet she was sad over leaving her
father. One minute she was crying and begging to stay with
him, and the next she was jumping up and down with joy
over the trip.

Early the next morning in the spring of 1848, the small
band left Humboldt Sink on their long journey. Scouts rode
ahead, followed by Chief Winnemucca and his best men.
Children rode behind their parents on their horses, and
babies nestled in baskets tied to their mothers' backs. Sarah
rode behind her older brother, Natchez.

Unlike the wagon trains that were piled high with
supplies and goods to sell and trade in California, Chief
Winnemucca's band traveled light. Each family had water
jugs, baskets for cooking and gathering food, and weapons
for hunting.

Progress was slow as they edged over the rough path
known as the California Trail. When they met a wagon
train, Chief Winnemucca would visit the white travelers'
camp and introduce himself. His letter from General

Frémont had a magical effect on the strangers. Scowls quickly turned to smiles followed by handshakes and friendly conversation. The whites often gave him gifts of food and clothing for his band. Sometimes he had to return to his camp for help in carrying the boxes of bread and beef. After each visit with his new friends, he would wave his slip of paper and smile broadly, telling his people that it had spoken for them.

Sarah enjoyed the food and admired the pretty calico dresses and flannel shirts the whites gave to her big sister Mary and brothers. But she was still afraid of white people. She hid inside the folds of her rabbit skin blanket every time they visited her camp. She connected white people with the scary hoots of owls heard in the night. Older Paiutes were fond of saying that the hoot of the owls was the voice of an old woman looking for children to eat. She carried a basket with spikes in the bottom, and if she heard a child crying, she would toss him in the basket and carry him away.

Sarah's curiosity finally got the better of her. One day while several white men were talking with Chief Winnemucca, she peeked out of her blanket to see what they really looked like. They didn't look at all like owls. They were really rather nice looking. From then on she smiled and tried to be friendly with the strangers.

Each day brought a new adventure for Sarah. She munched on white bread, sipped water from a cup, and rolled a lump of sugar around on her tongue. The sugar was the best thing she had ever tasted. The only sweet she had ever had before was the powdered honeydew that formed on the leaves of reeds.

Chief Winnemucca led them on, up and over the high

A street in Sacramento as it looked when Chief Winne-mucca's band visited the city.

Sierra Nevadas and down into the Sacramento Valley. They stayed in Sacramento for a few days and met Chief Winnemucca's friends living there. Like sightseers today, they gazed at the many interesting sights—the large stone houses and the big ships on the river. A few even went aboard one of the ships. Sarah was content to have Natchez tell her about what the ship was like.

Wonders never ceased for Sarah. In Stockton, California, a white woman gave her some calico dresses. She was thrilled with the colorful dresses for all her skirts were woven of long grasses and sagebrush bark. But, as soon as the woman left, her mother burned the dresses. They had belonged, Tuboitonie found out, to a little girl about Sarah's age who had died. The Paiutes burned the belongings of a dead person to keep his or her spirit from returning to claim them.

Sarah soon forgot her disappointment over not being able to wear the pretty dresses when she was invited to see the woman's home. It was a large, three-story house on a hill.

To Sarah, the shiny dining room table and its red upholstered chairs were the prettiest things she had ever seen. Even though her mother told her not to, she couldn't resist pulling herself up into one of the large chairs. The owner of the house told Tuboitonie it was all right, for her children ate at the table. Now Sarah felt that she understood why her grandfather admired the white people. They had so many marvelous things.

Sarah wanted to stay in Stockton, but her grandfather said they must go on to the San Joaquin Valley. One of his army friends had a large ranch there. They were given a big plot of land beside the San Joaquin River for their campsite.

On the ranch, the men and boys worked in the fields and orchards. They learned something about farming. Natchez and Tom, Sarah's brothers, herded horses and cattle in the hills. The women worked in the rancher's house as maids and cooks. Ranch women taught them and their daughters how to cook and sew.

Sarah happily explored the new world about her. She was a friendly, outgoing child and made friends instantly. She played games with the white children and taught them how to make mud animals and dolls and wreaths of flowers. She especially liked riding around the ranch in one of the big wagons. Sometimes she was allowed to sit up front with the driver.

The men and boys were content in California. They liked

their work on the ranch, and, as people who had never worked for money before, their small wages seemed generous. Even their fears of rifles disappeared. Their wives, mothers, and sisters, however, were homesick for their own land and people.

The women were afraid that their husbands and sons might be ambushed in the hills. Nothing the men said eased their concern. Other workers on the ranch paid too much attention to their pretty daughters, and they worried that white men might steal them.

Their fears turned to panic after a couple of men came to Tuboitonie's tent one night and asked her to give them Mary. The rancher invited her and her daughters to stay in his home with his family until the Paiute men came down from the hills.

Chief Winnemucca agreed to take them back to Nevada when the snow began to melt on the mountains. The night before they left, the ranch families had a party for the Paiutes. Feasting and gifts were exchanged. Beautiful blankets, clothing, and horses were given them. Now that they had many horses, they could be as proud as the Apaches.

Dressed in the flaming red shirt and a scarlet blanket across his shoulders, the stately old chief led his group back over the Sierras to Humboldt Sink. But, instead of a joyful homecoming, it was one of sadness. Many of their relatives and friends had died from a strange sickness that had come to the tribe while they were gone. They believed whites had poisoned their streams.

Chief Winnemucca tried to calm them. He was certain that the whites would not poison their own water supply.

The crowded gold fields of California.

Something else had brought the evil. Historians have identified the disease as cholera, which was spread by flies from a wagon train.

Traffic on the trail increased many times over that summer. Settlers eager to get to California to make new homes for themselves poured across the desert. They were not the only whites crossing Paiute lands. Gold had been discovered in California, and the Gold Rush of 1849 was at its peak. Adventurers hoping to dig their fortunes from the western slopes of the Sierra Nevadas followed the trail, too. As fond as Sarah had become of white people, the crowds terrified her.

They destroyed the balance of nature and completely changed the Paiutes' way of life. Their horses and cattle stripped the valleys of all growing things and used up the scant water supply. Their animals trampled the earth into a sodden mass, and their wagons cut deep ruts across the desert.

The Paiutes tried to be polite and friendly, but the impatient settlers and miners had no need of their friendship. They were apt to take pot shots at any Indians they saw. Since they passed through mostly in the spring and fall, the Paiutes continued gathering food, hunting, and fishing. They carefully avoided the paths of the wagon trains.

Chief Winnemucca managed to keep his tribe from striking back at the strangers. Finally, it became so dangerous for the Paiutes to stay near the whites that he led his people to the mountains for safety.

CHAPTER III

A Wise Man Dies

In April 1860, Chief Winnemucca lay dying in his wickiup. Signal fires were placed on nearby mountain tops to summon the tribe. They came from far and wide to pay their respects to their beloved leader. He gave over leadership of the Paiutes to Poito, who also became known as Chief Winnemucca. He asked Poito to take care of his people and to try to keep the peace with the whites. When he died on April 23, he was buried with his letter from General Frémont and the Bible the general had given him.

"I had a father, mother, brothers, and sisters; it seemed I would rather lose all of them than my poor grandpa," Sarah said when she told her story years later. "I was only a simple child, yet I knew what a great man he was. I mean great in principle. I knew how necessary it was for our good that he should live."

Sarah was sixteen years old. She was a pretty girl with an oval face, golden skin, and sparkling black eyes. She and her younger sister, Elma, had been living with Major Ormsby, manager of the stage line at Mormon Station, and his family. Thanks to Mrs. Ormsby's teaching, Sarah spoke English easily and felt at home among the white farmers who lived in the settlement. Making friends came easily to

The trading post at Mormon Station, the oldest white settlement in Nevada.

her, and her pleasing personality won over the whites.

Shortly before their grandfather's death, the girls had gone back to their people. Kind as the settlers had been to them, tempers had flared when two white men were killed on a mountain trail. The arrows of Washoe Indians had been found with their bodies. The angry farmers wanted to hang three Washoe men for the crime. Sarah pleaded with Mrs. Ormsby to help them, for she was sure they were innocent. The Washoes were about to be hung when suddenly they bolted and ran. All three of them were shot and killed. Little Elma was so upset that she cried herself sick, and the Ormsbys sent the two girls back to their family. A few weeks later, two white men confessed to the crime of which the Indians had been accused.

In spite of what had happened, the old chief still wanted

his granddaughters to have an education. Before he died, he asked Mr. Snyder, a white man who was a friend of his, to take the girls to a school in San Jose. Shortly afterwards, Sarah and Elma boarded the stage for the trip to California. Mr. Scott, another friend of their grandfather, met them in Sacramento, and the girls had a thrilling ride down the Sacramento River to San Francisco. After a few days of sight-seeing in the city, Mr. Scott took them to the St. Mary's Sisters of Charity School in San Jose.

The black-robed nuns were kind to the girls, and the other students made them feel welcome. Sarah and Elma did well in their classes. They especially liked sewing and embroidery and, of course, playing at recess. But they weren't allowed to stay at the school. Some of the parents didn't want their daughters to go to school with two Indians. After only three weeks, the nuns asked Mr. Scott to take them back to their family in Nevada. The dead chief's dream of having his granddaughters educated like his white friends had ended quickly. Nevertheless, Sarah understood the importance of an education. She followed the nuns' advice to study on her own, and over the years she often spent the money she earned buying books.

Sarah and Elma returned home to find the Paiutes deeply troubled. Silver had been discovered in the nearby Virginia Mountains a year earlier and had brought thousands of miners and settlers back over the Sierra Nevadas from California. The mining towns of Virginia City, Gold City, and Silver City sprang up almost overnight. The Paiutes watched with alarm as the whites drove out the game, fed the plants the Paiutes used for food to their mules, and cut down the pine nut trees to build shacks. Cyanide from the silver mines spilled into the rivers and killed the fish.

Chief Winnemucca II, Sarah's father, tried to keep the peace, but he was having trouble governing the tribe. The miners stole the Paiutes' ponies, and the Paiutes struck back by stealing the horses and cattle of the whites. Often the Paiutes stole just to keep from going hungry, for their other sources of food were being destroyed. Some worked around the mining camps, and many of the women, including Sarah, worked as servants in the towns. Their white employers often mistreated them.

One day two Paiute girls disappeared while gathering roots. Their families searched the entire area for them. They were finally found bound and gagged in the cellar of a house at William's Station outside Carson City. Natchez and several other men rescued the girls.

Now the anger of the Paiutes was at fever pitch, and they held a council of all the bands at Pyramid Lake to decide what to do. Chief Winnemucca sided with those who favored going to war, but as it turned out, the decision was no longer theirs.

While the Paiutes were in council, two white men were killed at William's Station. The settlers called it a massacre and demanded that the Indians be punished. Many in the settlement felt that the Paiutes had not committed the crime because they had always been peaceful. Even so, a group of about a hundred men, led by Major Ormsby, set out to find the Indians and punish them.

They followed the trail of the Paiutes along the Truckee River for about a hundred miles. On May 13, 1860, the first battle of the Paiute War was fought at a large meadow beside the river. Chief Winnemucca stationed his six

Chief Winnemucca II, Sarah's father.

hundred warriors in a semicircle on a low hill opposite the meadow. His men were completely hidden by the tall sagebrush. When the whites charged the hill, the Indians fell back. The settlers thought they had scored a victory only to discover that they were surrounded by the Indians on both sides.

Chief Winnemucca did not enter the battle himself. Splendidly dressed with a red and white sash flung over his broad shoulders and a white cap with plume on his head, he commanded his men from a rise nearby. Cooly and calmly he gave orders by raising and lowering a spear. The battle lasted only a few hours. The Paiutes lost only about twenty-five men while the settlers lost seventy. Major Ormsby was among those who were killed. Natchez made a desperate attempt to save the white man who had once been his friend, but the major was shot by a passing warrior as Natchez tried to help him.

When a second battle was fought a few weeks later, the Paiutes were no match for the professional soldiers who were sent from California. This time, they were forced to flee to the bleak and barren mountains in the north. Carrying their wounded with them, they stayed in the mountains with their families for the rest of the summer. They would not make peace until something definite was done about the settlers.

Meanwhile, the whites were doing something about the Paiutes. Fort Churchill was built on the Carson River to protect the settlers and the Pony Express. Land at Pyramid Lake was set aside as a Paiute reservation and Colonel Frederick Lander set up a meeting with Chief Winnemucca. He promised the chief that the U.S. government would give

Fort Churchill was built on the Carson River in 1860 to protect wagon trains, settlers, and miners from the Indians.

his people food and that they would be taught how to farm if they came to the reservation. The land around Pyramid Lake would be theirs.

The reservation was a troubled place from the beginning. Indian agents leased the land to ranchers and farmers. Government supplies were slow in coming, and the agents often sold the food and clothing that was supposed to be given to the Paiutes. No attempt was made to teach them how to raise their own food.

After a few years Paiutes began leaving the reservation. Some worked for ranchers, while others tried to survive by hunting and fishing. Many had to depend on hand-outs from settlers to live. A large number went to Oregon and Idaho where they could live by themselves in peace.

Sarah herself was working as a maid in Virginia City. Even so, she kept in close touch with her people and was troubled. She was upset by the reports that some of them were stealing, and her father seemed unable to stop them. On one visit home it became clear to her that he was too old and tired to give strong leadership. At a time when they needed a firm hand to guide them, their chief lacked the strength and will to provide it.

Sarah remembered the lessons her grandfather had taught her. He firmly believed that the Paiutes should learn to farm and take up the ways of the white people. She set out to persuade them to stop the looting, and she urged them to learn how to farm without the help of the Indian agent. When she was told that the whites were behaving even worse than they, she refused to accept it as an excuse. If they worked and tried to make a living for themselves, she was confident that everything would turn out all right.

Sarah also turned to the whites themselves. It was she who urged her father and brother to meet with the governor of the Nevada Territory, James W. Nye. Sarah acted as interpreter for the meeting—that is, she put her father's words into English for the governor. Chief Winnemucca asked him to stop the white squatters from carving out sections of the reservation land for their own use. He also wanted the governor to put an end to the Indian agents' leasing of reservation land to ranchers and farmers. Gov-

James W. Nye, governor of the Nevada Territory.

ernor Nye promised to do something about the situation right away. Sarah believed that he would keep his word and left the meeting with high hopes.

Sarah was only twenty years old, but already she had taken on the role of a leader. Thanks to her own efforts, she was well educated for a woman of her time. She knew the ways of the whites and their language, but more important, she knew her own people — and the land they came from — as the child and grandchild of Paiute chiefs.

CHAPTER IV

Help from the Army

As the months passed, nothing changed at Pyramid Lake. Governor Nye had forgotten his promises to Sarah and her father and brother.

Trouble between the settlers and Paiutes increased. When the Paiutes fought back by stealing horses and cattle to keep from starving, the settlers called in the army. Sometimes the settlers falsely accused the Indians of stealing so that the soldiers would come and buy their beef, grain, and horses for a good price.

Sarah's dreams for her people were punctured at almost every turn. Early one morning soldiers swept down upon a camp of Paiutes on a small lake. Chief Winnemucca and the men were away on a fishing trip. Only old men, women, and children were left at the camp. The soldiers had been sent to look for cattle thieves, but they didn't bother to ask questions. They opened fire at once and killed thirty-two persons in all. Among the dead was Sarah's baby brother. The only survivor was a sister, who was able to jump on a horse and ride away.

A few months later, Sarah's favorite uncle was killed by a settler who wanted his land. Her mother and older sister Mary died the next year.

Natchez Winnemucca, Sarah's brother.

Sarah was grieved and shocked. She left her job in Virginia City and went to live with Natchez on the reservation, where she shared the hard times. In Sarah's words, "I sta[y]ed with my brother all winter, and got along very poorly, for we had nothing to eat half of the time. Sometimes we would go to the agent's house and he would get my sister-in-law to wash some clothes, and then he would give us some flour to take home."

After the deaths in his family, Chief Winnemucca went to Oregon with a band of his followers. He left Natchez in charge of those living at Pyramid Lake, but the Indian agent was the real power there. Since the Bureau of Indian Affairs was in Washington, D.C., more than two thousand miles away, the agent could run things as he pleased. He completely ignored the promises made to the Paiutes when they agreed to come to the reservation.

Sarah had not been at Pyramid Lake long before she was at war with Newgent, the Indian agent. She objected fiercely to his selling timber and leasing reservation land to the whites. He stocked a store with food and clothing the Indian Bureau sent to be given to the Paiutes. He made them pay for their food and clothing with the little money they earned cutting hay and doing other jobs. They were constantly in debt to the agent. When Sarah complained about these things, Newgent called her a troublemaker.

When he began selling gunpowder to the Paiutes, Sarah knew there would be trouble. It wasn't long in coming. A Paiute who had wandered off the reservation put up a fight when soldiers tried to search him for gunpowder. The soldiers shot him. This looked like a plot to the Paiutes because the agent had sold him the gunpowder and he was killed for possessing it.

Sarah and Natchez learned there was a plot to kill the agent. As much as they hated Newgent, they knew that if he were killed, it would mean even more trouble for their people. They warned him and then tried to stop the plotters against the agent's life. Before they could reach the men, the brothers of the dead Paiute killed two white men for revenge.

Newgent and a group of settlers headed at once for Fort McDermitt to get the army. Sarah and Natchez waited anxiously for the troops to arrive at the reservation. The commander of Fort McDermitt, however, knew of their efforts to keep peace on the reservation. He invited them to come to the fort and talk about their problems.

This time, rather than acting as an interpreter, Sarah herself spoke for the Paiutes. She told the commander, Col.

Fort McDermitt, where the Paiutes came to be protected from the settlers.

James N. McElroy, how her people were being mistreated by the greedy agent and the settlers. He promised to send food and supplies at once to the hungry Paiutes. He would also send troops to protect them from the settlers.

Colonel McElroy then offered Sarah a job as interpreter at Fort McDermitt. Her salary would be sixty-five dollars a month and room and board. Even more wonderful, she could bring her people with her to Fort McDermitt. The fort that had been built to protect the settlers from the Indians was now offering refuge to the Indians from the whites.

The Paiutes welcomed the chance to get away from Newgent. Army troops went with them on the long journey from western Nevada to the northeastern corner of the state. Many walked because there were not enough horses for everyone. It took them twenty-eight days to climb up and down the rugged desert hills and valleys.

They were given a campsite on the edge of the fort, and each family had a large canvas tent. Every morning at dawn the women gathered to receive the day's food. Sarah helped happily in the busy routine of handing out beef and bread.

Her hopes soared. The Paiutes from Pyramid Lake were now comfortably settled and had plenty of food and clothing. She was eager to bring other members of the tribe to the fort. With Colonel McElroy's permission, she and Natchez contacted scattered bands and invited them to the fort. When she told them about the large canvas tents, free food, and kind treatment, they came gladly.

Colonel McElroy was especially eager to bring Chief Winnemucca to the base. The army was rounding up wandering bands of Indians, who faced being placed on reservations by force or being killed. He was concerned for the old Paiute chief's safety.

He offered to send some soldiers with Natchez to find Chief Winnemucca in his hideout in Oregon, but Natchez wanted to go alone.

Natchez rode his horse at full gallop most of the way. Following an old Paiute custom, he placed signal fires on mountain tops until he finally located his father's camp. Chief Winnemucca and his band returned with Natchez to the fort. Now there were nine hundred Paiutes living at Fort McDermitt.

They were happy on the army base. They fared better than at any other time since they lost their lands. Colonel McElroy was fair and just. He made sure that food, supplies, and jobs were handed out fairly. The men and boys earned money by tending cattle, cutting wood for fence posts, and building houses and fences. The women sewed and did household chores about the base and bought colorful calico for dresses with their small earnings. They gathered seeds and roots for winter and even held a pine nut festival. The colonel gave the men ammunition to use on a hunting trip.

There was one problem—at least from Chief Winne-mucca's point of view. He frowned on the way the young soldiers flirted with the Paiute girls. Most of all, he objected to the attention they paid to his pretty daughter. Natchez even asked the commander to order the soldiers not to talk to Sarah.

At first, Sarah tried to discourage the young men. She enjoyed dancing, however, and she found it hard to turn down invitations to the weekly dances at the base. Often she rode horseback across the plains or along the shady river with one, then another, of the young officers.

Her favorite riding companion was a handsome young cavalry officer from New York, Lt. Edward Bartlett. Sarah was taken with his lighthearted wit and charming manners. He, in turn, admired her for her intelligence, high spirits, and independence. The two rode together and went to the weekly dances. Chief Winnemucca and Natchez disap-proved strongly, but there was nothing they could do. They had known Lieutenant Bartlett at Pyramid Lake and remembered that he was fond of drinking. Furthermore, Chief Winnemucca did not believe that Paiutes and whites should marry.

When Bartlett received a transfer to Salt Lake City, the couple ran away together and were married on January 29, 1871. The marriage was stormy from the start. Bartlett drank heavily and sold some of Sarah's jewelry without her consent. After leading an active outdoor life, Sarah was unhappy keeping house in the city. Natchez showed up at her door one day with orders from their father for her to return home. Her husband was away at the time, and Sarah willingly returned to her family at Fort McDermitt.

She was back at her job only a short time when Colonel McElroy was transferred to another base. The new commander had little use for the Paiutes camped on the base and they began drifting away. When he cut off their food, the rest of the tribe left. Most of them returned to Pyramid Lake, and Sarah went with them.

Although the Paiutes had been well cared for at Fort McDermitt, Sarah knew that the only lasting solution to their problems was for them to learn how to earn their own living. She felt that farming was the best thing for them to do. If they learned how to grow their own food, they would not have to depend on the army or the government.

While at Fort McDermitt she had written the commissioner of Indian affairs in Washington, asking him to have someone teach farming to the Paiutes. Now she wrote to him again and asked that plots of farmland be assigned to them. Nothing came of her request. Meanwhile, the new agent at Pyramid Lake kept on leasing good farmland to the whites.

Sarah felt defeated. She was tired of trying to get help from selfish whites for her farming project. Her own people seemed resigned to giving up. They were unwilling to try farming on their own. She decided to get away from the many problems at Pyramid Lake and went north to visit her father in the Oregon wilderness.

CHAPTER V

A New Way of Life

In 1872 Malheur Reservation was set aside in eastern Oregon for, in the words of President Grant's order, "all the roving and straggling bands [of Indians] . . . which can be induced to settle there." Sarah had been with Chief Winnemucca for only a short time when her brother Lee brought her a letter from the agent at Malheur. He wanted to hire Sarah as an interpreter. At first it seemed to be the wrong job for Sarah. She wanted nothing more to do with Indian agents! Lee, however, kept after her, and finally she asked her father if he would go with her. The old chief agreed, and the three of them, along with Chief Winnemucca's band, arrived at Malheur in May 1875.

Sam Parrish, the Indian agent at Malheur, gave them a warm welcome. He told them he was their friend and would take care of them. Best of all, he said that he would teach them to farm.

Whatever doubts and fears Sarah had about coming to Malheur quickly vanished. To her surprise, Sam Parrish was a good agent.

There were no problems over shipments from the government. Parrish handed out food, clothing, and supplies as soon as he received them. He also gave each family a plot of land to farm. They could grow whatever crops they wished for their own use, and if they raised more than they needed, they could sell or trade it. As for other work, everyone was paid for his or her labor, no matter how small the job.

The reservation became a beehive of activity. The first summer that Sarah spent at Malheur, the men built a dam and dug a large irrigation ditch for their farm plots. They worked so hard and fast that they completed the 2½ mile long ditch in only six weeks. They also made a road across the reservation to make it easier to transport their crops. Some men cut timber for fences and a schoolhouse, while others cut hay and grain or cleared land for planting. A few were learning how to become blacksmiths and carpenters.

As a reward for a long summer of hard work, Parrish let the men go on a hunting trip. The Paiutes held a feast before the hunt and another upon their return. They stored the dried venison for the winter just the way they had done when roaming the Great Basin.

After the few winter crops were harvested, the men busied themselves making the soil ready for spring planting. Some planted barley and oats, while others chose watermelons, turnips, and potatoes for their crops. If a man grew only potatoes on his plot, he swapped the surplus for his friend's barley or turnips. Parrish furnished the hay for the horses, seeds, and plows.

It was a banner day when the schoolhouse was completed. Classes began in June 1876. Mrs. Charles Parrish, the agent's sister-in-law, was the teacher. Sarah was her assistant and taught English. On the first day of school, so many students came that Mrs. Parrish and Sarah had to arrange for classes to meet at different times of the day and week so everyone could attend. They taught reading, writing, arithmetic, and sewing.

The children loved singing most of all. Mrs. Parrish had brought a small organ with her to the reservation and played it for the children. Mothers of the children often came to the school to listen to the children sing. Sitting outside the schoolhouse windows, they clapped their hands to the music and frequently joined in.

It was a happy time for the Paiutes. When Sarah wasn't busy with her other duties, she often rode around the reservation to admire their growing crops. She would stop to praise them for their hard work. Life had never been better.

The only person unhappy with the life at Malheur Reservation was Oytes, a Paiute medicine man. He was jealous of Sam Parrish because of the respect the Paiutes had for the agent. Oytes made the Paiutes pay him part of their earnings by threatening to put a spell on them that would make them sick. He wouldn't work and did his best to keep others from working, too. Sarah talked with Oytes and tried to make him behave, but he wouldn't listen to her.

Finally Sam Parrish decided to put an end to his troublemaking. Oytes had boasted that a bullet couldn't kill him, and Parrish called his bluff. He offered to give Oytes three hundred dollars if he would let Parrish shoot at him. Oytes was terrified by Parrish's offer. Falling to his knees, he begged the agent to spare his life. He promised to do anything Parrish asked. From then on, he worked as everyone else did and didn't try to scare the Paiutes into giving him money.

The happiness at Malheur came to an end when word

Sam Parrish, the Indian agent at Malheur, who helped the Paiutes make the reservation a better place to live.

came that Parrish was to be replaced by another agent, R.V. Rinehart. The Paiutes knew of Rinehart's dishonest ways because he ran a store in the nearby village of Stone City. Not only did he sell shoddy goods, but he also sold the Indians whiskey even though it was against the law.

Sarah did everything she could to keep Rinehart from coming to Malheur. She wrote to everyone she knew in high official positions to protest his appointment. If Parrish couldn't stay, she pleaded, at least send somebody who was honest and would continue to help them. Nothing came of her efforts, and Rinehart arrived in the summer of 1876.

He lost no time in letting the Indians know that he was boss. He informed them that the reservation belonged to the government, and since he was the government's representative, they would do exactly as he said. If they didn't like the way he did things, they could leave. The Paiutes were shocked. They thought of Malheur as their own land and were trying to learn how to make a living on it.

Rinehart took away the farmers' crops and gave them only a small portion for their own use. The rest he sold to the villagers or gave to his relatives. The Paiutes no longer had control of the crops they raised or the land on which they raised them. Instead, Rinehart paid the Paiutes wages out of the goods the government sent.

Blankets were valued at six dollars and hats at five dollars. Even food was included in their wages. When everything was added up, a worker might receive only two dollars in cash on payday. The Paiutes grumbled among themselves and to Sarah. Why should they have to work for the things the government sent them?

The Paiutes grew restless and discontented. Food issues were made more and more rarely. Only those with wage-credits were allowed to receive food. Anyone who was too old to work or had not worked at an assigned job went hungry.

Many of the people wanted to leave the reservation, but Sarah persuaded them to stay. They would suffer more in the settlements where they weren't wanted in the first place. She began writing letters to people of importance in the government and in the army. She begged them to remove Rinehart.

The final blowup between Rinehart and Sarah came the day she presented him with a long list of the Paiutes' complaints. He burst into a rage, shouting that if the Paiutes didn't like the way he ran Malheur, they could all leave. He fired Sarah on the spot and ordered her off the reservation. Just to annoy him, she stayed three weeks longer.

Very determined and dedicated to her cause, Sarah turned her thoughts toward Washington, D.C. Letter writing had done nothing for her people, but perhaps a trip to present their problems with Rinehart would. Her father encouraged her to go and so did the rest of her tribe. They even took up a collection among themselves to help pay her expenses. Two men who had heard of her trip east offered to pay her fifty dollars to take them to Silver City, Idaho. One of the men, a widower, had a little girl who was going with them.

Sarah and her three companions set out in her buckboard wagon on June 8, 1878. She planned to sell her wagon in Silver City and with her passengers' fares and the Paiutes' collection buy a train ticket to Washington, D.C.

She paid little attention to her passengers bracing themselves against the jolts of the wagon. Time was all that counted. The little girl took an instant liking to Sarah. So did her father. Before they were halfway to Silver City, he had proposed marriage to Sarah. She was in no mood for romance and certainly not marriage. Her mind was on getting them to Silver City as soon as possible and boarding a train for the nation's capital.

After Sarah left the reservation, the Paiutes began leaving, too. Now that she was gone, there was no one to help them deal with the hateful Rinehart. Some bands had already slipped away to hunt and fish to keep from starving. Oytes persuaded Chief Winnemucca and his band of several hundred to leave Malheur and go with him and Leggin. Oytes led them to a barren stretch on the Malheur River.

No sooner had they arrived than they were met by a war party of Bannock Indians. For a long time certain elders of the tribes in the area had been urging all Indians to rise up against the whites. Now was the time, they said, to get rid of the whites once and for all. The news spread from tribe to tribe in the Northwest.

The Bannocks were the angriest among them. They claimed the Big Camas Prairie near the Fort Hall reservation in Idaho as their land. The settlers' hogs, cattle and horses were destroying the camas fields. The camas was a lily with a sweet root that the Bannocks prized as food.

In May 1878 the Bannocks began the war that they had been planning for a year. Some of the Paiutes and Columbia River Indians joined in the uprising.

Chief Winnemucca and his people wanted no part of the Bannocks' war. They refused to join them. With the help of Oytes, the Bannocks took away their weapons and made them their prisoners. The Paiutes were now in danger not only from the Bannocks, but also from the army. General Oliver Howard, commander of the Western Forces, was already rushing from his headquarters to put down the Indian rebellion.

As Sarah and her passengers jostled over the rocky Idaho roads, they wondered about the empty houses they passed. On the fourth day of their journey, they met three men on the road who told them about the Bannock War. The men urged them to hurry on to Stone House, a sturdy storehouse on the stage road, where the settlers' families were gathered for safety. "They [the Bannocks] want nothing more than to kill Chief Winnemucca's daughter," they told her.

At Stone House Sarah learned the true scope of the war. The Bannocks were killing everyone—Paiutes as well as settlers—said one Indian scout who had fought them. She offered her help at once to Captain Reuben Bernard, who was on his way with a company of soldiers to Sheep Ranch. There he would set up an army command post. "If I can be of any use to the army," she said, "I am at your service, and I will go with it till the war is over."

The captain wanted to use her as a guide since she knew the country well and promised that he would ask General Howard's permission. He told her to meet him at Sheep Ranch and left with his soldiers.

Sarah herself was kept at Stone House, and she spent a sleepless night. The settlers believed that her wagon was carrying ammunition to the hostile Indians. The soldiers refused to search the wagon and put a guard on it to protect it from the angry whites. The next morning Sarah herself showed the people that there was nothing of value to the Indians in her buckboard. She was able to leave when four Indians and a white man passed through on their way to the command post at Sheep Ranch.

They rode at a fast gallop for most of the thirty-mile trip. As they came close to the army camp, a guard opened fire on them. He didn't even stop when he saw that the five Indians were in the company of a white person.

Side by side and shouting like warriors, Sarah and the white man rode down on the guard as he started to run towards the camp. "I tell you," Sarah wrote in her book, "we very soon made him stop his foolishness."

It was a fitting beginning to the most daring and dangerous experience of Sarah's life.

CHAPTER VI

Army Scout

When Sarah joined the soldiers at Sheep Ranch, Captain Bernard was calling for volunteers to find the Bannock camp. No scout, Indian or white, wanted to take such a risk. Capture by the Bannocks would mean certain death. Besides, the trip would take them through some of the most rugged country in the West. The most experienced scout could get lost and starve in the mountains where even the hardy sagebrush grew only in scattered clumps.

Two Paiutes, John and George, were willing to go anywhere but near the Bannock camp. They told Sarah about three white men who had escaped from the Bannocks with Natchez, Sarah's brother. Natchez's horse had fallen exhausted in the chase, and Natchez himself must be dead. It was then that Sarah decided she would go—alone.

General Howard gave his permission, and Captain Bernard wrote a letter for her to carry. It would let any whites she came across know that she was on army business. Now that John and George saw that she could not be talked out of looking for the Bannocks, they agreed to go with her.

They left Sheep Ranch June 13, 1878. Sarah took the lead as they headed for the Owyhee River, fifteen miles away.

They passed the spot where a stage driver had been ambushed only two days before. His whip was lying by the side of the road.

On the other side of the river they picked up a fresh trail. It led them to the place where the Bannocks had camped while fighting at South Mountain a few days earlier. Their war chief, Buffalo Horn, was killed in the battle, and signs of mourning were strewn about the ground. Clumps of hair, broken beads, and torn clothing were all about. Now the Bannocks would be even angrier as they tried to avenge the death of their leader.

Sarah's horse stumbled and lost its footing as it scrambled over beds of rock. They stopped to rest a short time at a farmhouse owned by one of Sarah's friends. It was deserted—the only signs of life about the place were squawking chickens. The house had been stripped of furniture, bedding, and clothing, and everything had been burned. The Paiutes' sharp eyes spotted footprints recently made by the Bannocks.

When they came to a fork in the road, they found a newly blazed trail leading straight into the mountains. John and George wanted to turn back, but Sarah insisted that they must go on. Along the trail they found signs that the Bannocks had gone before them. By the side of the path they found a clock and a fiddle that had, no doubt, once belonged to settlers killed or taken captive by the Bannocks.

The trail became steeper and rougher. It wound along huge granite slopes and ledges that jutted out over deep gorges and led them through rocky desert valleys at the foot of the mountains. John killed a mountain sheep, and they ate some of the meat and took some along with them. They

Rugged Steen's Mountain, where the Paiutes were held captive.

had eaten only hard bread washed down with a little water since they left Sheep Ranch the day before.

A few miles beyond Juniper Lake, Sarah happened to look up at Steen's Mountain, a jagged peak in the distance. There were two people running along one of the slopes. As they came closer, she recognized one of them as her youngest brother, Lee.

Lee told her that the Bannocks had taken her father and the Malheur Reservation Paiutes prisoner. They had taken away their blankets, weapons, and horses. Every day the

Bannocks told them they would kill anyone who tried to escape and, Lee said, they might already have killed Natchez. It was not until some time later that the Winnemucca family learned Natchez was safe at Fort McDermitt. Lee begged Sarah to go back. She would be killed if she was caught stealing into the camp.

Sarah was not about to give up now. She and her companions quickly changed from their white people's clothes to Indian dress. They took blankets and paint from their saddlebags and in a few seconds looked like Bannocks.

The Bannock camp was behind Steen's Mountain. Leading their horses, they climbed its steep slopes from the north side. Here the surface was so rough and rocky that the Bannocks had not bothered to place lookouts. The four Paiutes crawled on their hands and knees over the rock boulders. Knifelike edges of rock cut their hands and legs. They clung to short, scrubby brush to keep from losing their footing.

At a high point on the mountain's side, Sarah looked down upon the huge Bannock camp below. There were more than three hundred lodges and four hundred fifty warriors. Lee pointed out their father's lodge and those of the Paiutes.

They tied their horses to trees and started down the mountain on foot. Lee rushed ahead to scout for them. He would let Sarah know when it was safe for her to follow. Clinging to bushes, hiding behind rocks and trees, Sarah, John, and George made it down the mountain.

When darkness fell, Lee whistled softly. It was a signal they had used as children. Leaving the others hidden in the brush, Sarah crept inside the Bannock camp. When she located her father's tent, she gathered up a load of firewood and darted inside.

At first, Chief Winnemucca was afraid to leave the enemy camp, but Sarah convinced him that he would be in even greater danger if he stayed. The army would protect them if they went with her.

While the Bannocks were having their evening meal, the Paiutes crept out of camp, a few at a time. The women carried ropes as if they were going for wood. Chief Winnemucca and his nephews left the lodge last with Sarah. Although she had spoken bravely to her family, Sarah was exhausted and terrified. This is the way she described her escape in her book:

> My brother Lee jumped up, rope in hand, and went out of the tent, and then my father gave orders to his nephews and we four started out, leaving father's lodge all lonely. It was like a dream. I could not get along at all. I almost fell down at every step, my father dragging me along. Oh, how my heart jumped when I heard a noise close by. It was a horse running towards us. We had to lie down close to the ground. It came close to us and stopped. . . . I thought whoever it was would hear my heart beat.

The mysterious rider who discovered Sarah was Mattie, her sister-in-law. Worried that Sarah might drop from exhaustion, Lee had sent his wife back into camp with a horse for her. He and some of the men had seized the horses the Bannocks had stolen from them.

Tired as she was, Sarah led the procession over the mountain. The Paiute band traveled all night until they came to Juniper Lake. But no sooner had they stopped to rest than a scout rode up and told them the Bannocks were coming. They had fired at Lee, who was acting as rear guard for the last of the Paiutes to slip out of camp. Fortunately, they had missed him.

Chief Winnemucca gave orders that they ride two by two and keep close together. They rode as fast as they could, but their progress was too slow to suit Sarah. With John, George, and Mattie, she left her father with the group and dashed ahead to Sheep Ranch, about seventy miles away, to get the army.

By the time she reached Sheep Ranch late in the afternoon of June 15, Sarah was so exhausted she could hardly speak. For three days and two nights, she had ridden almost nonstop with very little sleep, food, and water. She had followed the trail of the Bannocks from southwestern Idaho to eastern Oregon—a distance of two hundred and twenty miles. As soon as Sarah reported on her mission, General Howard sent troops to lead Chief Winnemucca's band to safety at Fort Lyon.

More than a hundred of the last group of Paiutes to escape from the camp had been overtaken by Bannock warriors. Among them were the bands of Egan and Leggin. Egan's band joined the Bannocks in the war and fought with them. He became one of their war chiefs, as did Oytes, the man who had led Chief Winnemucca and his people to the place where they had been captured.

Sarah was very proud of what she had done. In her book she wrote: "This was the hardest work I ever did for the government in all my life. . . . Yes, I went for the government when the officers could not get an Indian man or a white man to go for love or money. I, only an Indian woman, went and saved my father and his people."

The soldiers and her people hailed her as a hero. Newspapers of the day ran stories about her bravery. The army promised her a reward of five hundred dollars for her bold rescue of her father and her people. She didn't have time to collect it.

General Howard asked her to be his personal interpreter, messenger, and guide. Mattie was to go with her. "I want you and Mattie with the headquarters," said General Howard. Sarah's information about the site of the Bannock camp, the number of warriors there, and how to reach it gave the army its first chance to put down the rebellion. General Howard changed his original plans and ordered all his troops to move against the Bannocks at Steen's Mountain.

For the next six weeks the Bannocks led the cavalry over the rugged peaks and hot alkaline deserts of eastern and central Oregon. Sarah all but lived in the saddle. She galloped from one cavalry unit to the next to deliver General Howard's dispatches. At night she read the Bannocks' signal fires on distant mountains and reported their messages to General Howard. After a battle she helped care for the injured Indians and soldiers.

Once a small cavalry unit was almost in panic when scouts reported the enemy on the next cliff. Even the officers with their fieldglasses said they could see them. Sarah studied the cliff through narrowed eyes. She burst into laughter. There were no Bannocks on the cliff. To give

General Oliver O. Howard, for whom Sarah worked as messenger and guide. General Howard had lost his arm at the Battle of Bull Run in the Civil War.

themselves time to get away, they had arranged rocks on the mountain peak to look like men.

The war continued through most of the summer of 1878. The swift Indians led the cavalry under General Howard's command on a wild chase through the Blue Mountains. The cavalry found it difficult to keep up with them, for they had to haul heavy guns and equipment across mountain peaks and up steep canyons. Sometimes the pack mules lost their footing and fell backwards into the river hundreds of feet below.

Sarah had good reason to be loyal to the army, and yet she had a great deal of respect for the courage and fighting skill of the Bannocks. And since she had grown up in wild country such as this, she had known the kind of freedom the enemy was fighting for. As she remembered a skirmish near Birch Creek, she said in her book, "Oh, what a feeling I had just before the fight came on. . . . Then the bugle sounded 'Fire!' I heard the chiefs singing as they ran up and down the front line as if it was only a play, and on our side was nothing but the reports of the great guns. All my feeling was gone. I wanted to go to them."

The white settlers who feared for their lives from the Bannocks wanted all Indians killed, whether they were peaceful or not. Unlike the brave soldiers she admired, some of the settlers who were fighting with the army ran away under fire. In this battle, Sarah thought she saw a strange bond between the warriors and the soldiers:

> Sometimes I laugh when I think of this battle. It was very exciting in one way, and the soldiers made a splendid chase, and deserved credit for it; but where was the killing? I sometimes think it was more play than anything else. If a white settler showed himself he was sure to get a hit from an Indian; but I don't believe they ever tried to hit a soldier,—they liked them too well,—and it certainly was remarkable that with all these splendid firearms, and the Gatling gun, and General Howard working at it, and the air full of hot bullets, and the ground strewn with cartridges, not an Indian fell that day.

*One of the earliest photos taken of "Princess" Winne-
mucca, as Sarah was called by the reporters who covered the
Bannock War.*

The army's goal throughout the campaign was to stop the Bannocks from killing the settlers and destroying their property. Finally, Egan, who had replaced Oytes as their war chief, was killed by a member of the Umatilla tribe for a reward offered by the settlers. Soon after Egan's death, the Bannocks gave up. They were taken by the troops to the Yakima Reservation in Washington.

Throughout the Bannock War, newspapers carried headlines about Sarah's bravery. Reporters who followed the conflict on horseback praised her daring and courage. Since they kept a safe distance during a battle, their stories were often based on rumors. On one occasion the newspapers printed that "Princess Winnemucca had been killed in battle." Her family was grief stricken.

A short time later Sarah made a visit to see her father at Fort McDermitt, where his band had camped during the war. He was overcome with relief and made her a chief because she had saved so many lives. This was a title never before given to a woman.

General Howard praised her, too. He described her as "courageous, intelligent, and a capable scout and interpreter."

Still, when plans were made for the Paiutes at the end of the war, Sarah was once again misled by the government.

CHAPTER VII

Broken Promises

When the Bannock War came to an end in September 1878, the Indian Bureau ordered the Paiutes to go back to the Malheur Reservation under army guard. Alarm spread through their camp. Those who had been trapped by the Bannocks were especially fearful of returning north. About half of them agreed to go to Malheur, while the rest decided to take their chances on escaping both the army and the settlers.

Early in October several hundred Paiutes, the Winnemucca family among them, left Fort McDermitt for Malheur. They stopped at Fort Harney to rest, and as their stay stretched from weeks into months, Sarah became worried. Winter was coming on, and travel would be very difficult.

She learned only a week before Christmas that they were being sent to the Yakima Reservation in southern Washington. Sarah was furious. Bannock prisoners were being held at Yakima, and the lives of her people would be greatly endangered, especially those who had escaped from the Bannock camp at Steen's Mountain.

She begged the commanding officer at Fort Harney not to send them to Yakima. But, if they must go, she asked him to let them wait until spring. Many would surely freeze in the biting cold. Since the orders had come from the commissioner of Indian affairs, who was head of the Indian Bureau, he could do nothing except send them on their way, guarded by his troops. Settlers had pressured the Indian Bureau to pen them up far away for they wanted to be rid of all Indians, even the peaceful Paiutes.

The Paiutes were panic stricken when they heard of the change in plans. They accused Sarah of selling out to the whites. Many tried to escape but were dragged back by the soldiers. Sarah and Mattie, Lee's wife, tried to keep them from trying to run away for they would freeze in the deep snow.

They were given only one week to get ready, and Sarah and Mattie worked around the clock to find warm clothing for the long journey. The army provided overcoats, boots, and shoes for the men, but there was nothing for the women. Sarah and Mattie had to find what they could— blankets, gloves, and odd pieces of clothing—for the shivering women. They lined the women's shoes and moccasins with pieces of fur.

On January 1, 1879, more than five hundred Paiutes started out for the much-dreaded Yakima Reservation. The fifty wagons that the government provided to carry them and their belongings were not nearly enough. A lucky few had horses, but many were forced to struggle through the snow on foot.

Temperatures dropped below zero as the Indians plodded across wind-swept mountains. Blizzards occurred almost daily, adding fresh snow. Newborn babies died at birth, and often their young mothers died, too. Old people suffered the most because they couldn't keep up with the rest. They stumbled and fell in the deep snow, unable to rise to their feet again. Many small children also died from the intense cold. An attempt was made to bury the bodies, but many were left where they had fallen. More than one hundred people died on the long march.

The starving, half-frozen Paiutes reached the Yakima Reservation on the last day of January. No one there had known that they were coming, and there was only enough food in the reservation's warehouses for the Indians already living there. The Indian agent quickly sent off a request for extra supplies. While there was nothing at Yakima to feed the Paiutes when they arrived, the Malheur warehouses were bulging with food and clothing. There wasn't a single Indian at Malheur Reservation.

Conditions were even worse than Sarah had feared. There was no food or clothing and not much shelter for her suffering people. They were housed in long, narrow sheds like those used for livestock. There was no firewood to build fires, and icy winds swept through the cracks in the walls.

Among those who died that year from the cold and lack of food and medical care was little Mattie, Sarah's sister-in-law. They were very close and had gone through the Bannock War together. Sarah and Lee, Mattie's husband, buried her. Sarah vowed that when she got her five-hundred-dollar reward from the army, she would do something about the condition of her people. She would let the public know how they were treated at Yakima.

Sarah saw her chance when the agent, a man named Wilbur, decided to hold a religious revival meeting at the reservation. He had been appointed to his post by a church board and claimed to be very religious. Wilbur invited an important preacher and several others from the East to lead the services. The day the visitors arrived at the agent's house, they were shocked to find a group of gaunt, half-naked Indians camped at the front door. That evening and every evening while the services lasted, Sarah paraded a large group of her poorly clothed people down the aisle to the front of the revival tent. The agent was furious with her. He had told the Paiutes to stay away from the revival meeting. He was embarrassed to have his guests see how wretched they really were.

Sarah had made her point. Word about the starving, ragged Indians at Yakima soon spread. And when she received her reward, she set out on a lecture tour.

Although she had not stood up before large groups of people before, Sarah had been making speeches for years. She had spoken for her people in dealings with Indian agents and high-ranking army officers. She also cared, and that caring touched the white people who listened to her now. One man, a Belgian doctor who heard her lecture in San Francisco, wrote in his journal that her emotion moved many of her listeners to tears.

Sarah described the Paiutes' suffering on their forced march in the dead of winter. She told about their troubles at Yakima. She blasted the Indian Bureau for its indifference to the Paiutes' needs and explained the ways the Indian agents cheated them. As she did all this, she named Rinehart, Wilbur, and the Indian commissioner.

Sarah's bold criticisms of the Indian Bureau alarmed the officials in Washington, D.C. More to quiet Sarah than anything else, they invited her to the nation's capital. Chief

The Winnemucca family (from left to right): Sarah, Chief Winnemucca II, and Natchez.

Winnemucca, Natchez, and Sarah's cousin Joe went, too, and the government paid for their trip.

Sarah was delighted to be able to give a firsthand report on the agents and the conditions of her people. They arrived in the capital early in January, 1880. They were hardly settled in their hotel rooms before Sarah suspected the real reasons for their invitation.

An Indian Bureau guide barely let them out of his sight. They could not go anywhere without him. Sarah was ordered not to talk to the press or make any speeches. The guide kept them on a steady round of sight-seeing from early morning until late at night. According to Sarah, they saw everything in the city except the old men's home.

Sarah and her party finally had a meeting with the

secretary of the interior, Carl Schurz. He was the cabinet member responsible for the Indian Bureau and, of course, the Indian commissioner, too. The only person of higher rank who could do anything about the Paiutes' problems was the president himself. Secretary Schurz promised to grant everything Sarah wished for the Paiutes if she would not make any speeches. He signed an order granting the Paiutes at Yakima permission to leave the hated reservation and return to Malheur. Each family at Malheur would receive a plot of land to farm. Those Paiutes who were already earning their living among the whites could remain where they were.

Eventually, Sarah and her party had a chance to meet President Rutherford B. Hayes. The meeting was brief. The

President Rutherford B. Hayes, whom the Winnemuccas met on their trip to Washington, D.C.

president shook their hands and greeted them. When Sarah told him that they had received the order from Secretary Schurz, he left the room.

With Chief Winnemucca sporting a new suit which the bureau had bought for him, the group boarded the train for Nevada. Sarah clutched the precious piece of paper from Secretary Schurz to her breast. She could hardly wait to spread the good news among her people.

There was no good news for the Paiutes at Yakima. Agent Wilbur refused to honor the order because, he said, it hadn't been addressed to him. Sarah pleaded and begged him to release her people. He stormily refused, and she became so angry that he threatened to have her thrown in jail. Sarah almost preferred jail to having to tell her people that she had failed in her mission. Many of the Paiutes at Yakima tried to escape, but Wilbur had them hunted down and brought back by force.

Not one of the promises made in the secretary's order was kept. Sarah felt defeated.

CHAPTER VIII

The Story Is Told

Sarah did not speak out for her people again for three years. She taught for a short time at a school for Indian children and then went to visit her sister Elma in Montana. While she was staying at the ranch which Elma and her wealthy husband owned, she met and married Lambert Hopkins, a white man who worked for the army. On the face of it, Sarah seemed to have put the troubles of the Paiutes behind her.

She had not forgotten them. Sarah kept on writing letters to the officials in Washington and urged her friends in the army to do so, too. Somehow word of the Paiutes' suffering reached the Peabody sisters in Boston. They asked Sarah to give a series of lectures in their city.

Sarah had reason to be hopeful for the first time since she had gone to Washington. The Peabody sisters, Elizabeth Palmer Peabody and Mary Peabody Mann, were two women who could bring her cause before people who were able and willing to help her. Both were published writers. Elizabeth Peabody, in fact, had been the first woman publisher in Boston. She had published Henry David Thoreau's "Civil Disobedience" in 1849. A hundred years later this famous essay guided the thinking of great leaders

Lambert H. Hopkins, the man Sarah married in 1882.

in human rights like Mahatma Gandhi and Martin Luther
King. Elizabeth and Mary had spoken on behalf of black
people when blacks were slaves in the South before the Civil
War. Now Elizabeth was working for women's right to vote,
a right they did not gain until 1920. The sisters were part of a
network of writers, thinkers, and ordinary people who, like
themselves, believed in human rights.

Elizabeth asked Sarah and Lambert to stay in her home
while they were in Boston, and she eagerly introduced them
to her friends. She didn't give her guests much time for
sight-seeing, however. Elizabeth devoted all her time to

Elizabeth P. Peabody, who made Sarah's lecture tour in the East possible.

making arrangements for Sarah's speeches. She rushed around renting halls, making lecture dates, and letting people know about Sarah, whom she called the "Indian Princess."

Thanks to her efforts, the lecture halls were always jammed. Sarah held an audience spellbound from the moment she opened her mouth to speak. Just as in San Francisco, her story about the government's broken promises and the Indian Bureau's neglect made her high-minded listeners gasp.

She told them that her people were peace loving, and

over and over again she stressed that the Paiutes didn't want charity. They wanted only a place to live without fear of being moved, a place where they would have a chance to make a living for themselves. She told of her work as an army scout, and although she blasted the Indian Bureau, she heaped praise on the army. Soldiers did not cheat Indians, she said. If they must live under supervision, let the army provide it.

Sarah also told the Bostonians about her people's ways. She described their customs and traditions and sang some of their songs. Since she no longer had skirts of woven grass, she wore a deerskin dress to remind people that her American heritage was different from theirs.

Before long, Sarah had invitations to speak in other eastern cities. During the year she lived in Boston, she spoke in Rhode Island, Connecticut, New York, and Pennsylvania, as well as Massachusetts.

Mary Peabody Mann thought that even more people should have a chance to learn Sarah's point of view. Mary had been married to Horace Mann, an educational reformer, and had written a book about her famous husband. She wanted Sarah to write the story of her life, and she offered to help. Somehow Sarah managed to squeeze in the time she needed to write. Mary edited her book and gave special attention to Sarah's poor spelling.

When officials in the Indian Bureau found out that Sarah was writing a book, they decided to fight back. If they couldn't stop her from putting her story in print, at least they could make sure that no one would believe her. Years earlier, when Sarah was at Malheur, Rinehart had written an angry attack on her in his report to the bureau. Now the

*Sarah in the deerskin dress in which she spoke to the people
of Boston.*

Mary Peabody Mann, who urged Sarah to write the book that told the story of the Paiutes' suffering.

Indian Bureau published the report in their magazine, *Council of Fire*, and sent copies to people who supported the Paiute cause.

The attempt of the Indian Bureau to blacken Sarah's name failed completely. Instead, the people of Boston and others who had known her rose to her defense. A host of army officers, judges, and government officials wrote letters praising her and agreeing with her stand on the Paiute problem.

When *Life Among the Paiutes: Their Wrongs and Claims* was published in 1883, it included some of those letters. There were even letters from the War Department, which was in charge of the army, to the Department of the Interior, which was in charge of the Bureau of Indian Affairs. Officials in the Indian Bureau resented the interference no end, and there is little doubt that the army's efforts made them more stubborn. Here were their letters for all to see and here, too, was a frank account of the suffering that had caused the protest.

All in all, the storm over *Life Among the Paiutes* boosted its sales and increased the number of Sarah's supporters. But for Sarah, there was no going back to the Indian Bureau for help. She had to find another way to deal with the American government.

There still was Congress. In a request called a petition, Sarah asked the Congress of the United States to pass a law for the Paiutes. In her petition Sarah said that her people, who once lived in the greater part of Nevada, now were one third fewer in number because of their "sufferings and wrongs." She asked Congress to give Malheur Reservation back to them and in so doing, prevent white settlement on their land. She also asked that those living at Yakima against their will be allowed to return to Malheur as Secretary Schurz had ordered. Thousands of citizens signed Sarah's petition, and it was brought before Congress by one of the representatives from Massachusetts.

Malheur was not to be theirs. The Indian Bureau no longer used it as a reservation, and it had been opened up to white settlement. But in July 1884, Congress passed a law granting land on the Pyramid Lake Reservation to members of Chief Winnemucca's band. Land at Pyramid Lake was also set aside for the Paiutes at Yakima and those who had fled from there.

Sarah and Lambert returned to Nevada a few weeks later, and Sarah received a hero's welcome. She went around the state visiting her people and spreading the good news that their loved ones would soon be coming home from Yakima. The only sad note in Sarah's homecoming was that her father was not there to greet her. Chief Winnemucca had died in 1882 at the age of ninety-five.

Sarah learned that getting a law passed was not the same thing as having it enforced. Secretary Schurz refused to carry out the law that Congress had passed for the Paiutes. He did nothing to enforce the Paiutes' land claims nor to help those kept at Yakima.

The disappointed Paiutes blamed Sarah for listening to a bunch of smooth talkers. Sarah herself felt that she was a failure and that her twenty-year struggle had come to nothing. With help from the Peabody sisters and their friends, she opened a school for Indian children on Natchez's farm near Lovelock, Nevada.

Sarah taught English, reading, writing, and sewing to her twenty-five students. She also taught them to honor their tribal traditions and culture. News of her success attracted visitors, including inspectors from the Indian Bureau. They were very impressed with the progress the children were making. Even so, Sarah and Elizabeth were unable to obtain government funds for the school. Sarah dreamed of having a boarding school and training students to become teachers, but this dream, like many in the past, never came true. The Peabody School lasted for only two years.

Lambert died in October, 1887, from tuberculosis. Four years later, on October 16, 1891, Sarah died from the same disease at her sister's home in Monida, Montana, where she had lived after closing her school. She was buried at Henry's Lake, Montana.

The United States did not listen to Sarah's message, but the Paiute nation paid attention to her words. In the years to come her people fought for their rights with the weapons that she, of all the Paiutes, was the first to use. Today, when problems arise, the Paiutes air them in court and in the newspapers. They have fought hard legal battles over their water rights to Pyramid Lake.

For hundreds of years the cutthroat trout living in the lake were one of their main sources of food and income. The trout disappeared after the Derby Dam was built over the Truckee River in 1905. The once clear lake water became salty, and over the years the water level dropped by ninety feet.

The Paiutes took their case to court to get more water before their lake became little more than a muddy pond. Since the 1960s they've waged an almost continuous fight. In the last ten years or so, the courts have ordered the water level raised. Each year the lake is stocked with fish, but the cutthroat trout is gone forever.

Now the Paiutes face other problems. Developers are eager to use the land around Pyramid Lake. Already it is a favorite spot for tourists who enjoy fishing.

There are about nine hundred Paiutes living on the Pyramid Lake Reservation. Many young people left when the Bureau of Indian Affairs began a relocation program in 1952 to bring Indians into the mainstream of American life.

Many of those who went to live in the city have since returned. They have found that they prefer their own way of life to the city's hustle and bustle. As a result, the relocation program was stopped in the fall of 1980.

Making a living on the desert reservation is far from easy. It is estimated that more than half of the Paiutes earn less than two thousand dollars a year. They raise cattle, fish, and sell fishing and camping licenses to tourists. Like those who have gone before them, they depend on the land for survival. And they are doing their best to keep that land unspoiled. Sarah would have been proud of them.

THE AUTHOR

Doris Kloss is a former history teacher who is a widely published free-lance writer with more than a hundred magazine articles to her credit. She received her bachelor's degree from Georgia College and her master's degree in history and political science from Duke University and has done further course work in journalism at UCLA and New York City College. *Sarah Winnemucca: The Story of an American Indian* is her first book. She notes that Sarah Winnemucca has been largely forgotten today although she was nationally known in her time and the most influential Paiute woman in history. In writing the biography of this native American leader, Ms. Kloss has made abundant use of primary research materials.

Photographs reproduced through the courtesy of the California State Library; the Nevada Historical Society; the Oregon Department of Transportation; the University of Nevada Library, Reno; and the Smithsonian Institution.

OTHER BIOGRAPHIES
IN THIS SERIES ARE

William Beltz
Robert Bennett
Black Hawk
Crazy Horse
Charles Eastman
Geronimo
Oscar Howe
Pauline Johnson
Ishi
Chief Joseph
Little Turtle
Maria Martinez
George Morrison
Daisy Hooee Nampeyo
Michael Naranjo
Osceola
Powhatan
Red Cloud
Will Rogers
John Ross
Sacagawea
Sealth
Sequoyah
Sitting Bull
Maria Tallchief
Tecumseh
Jim Thorpe
Tomo-chi-chi
Pablita Velarde
William Warren
Alford Waters
Annie Wauneka
Wovoka